Little Rabbit Lost

HARRY HORSE

PEACHTREE
ATLANTA

For Jessica and Ben

Ω

Published by
PEACHTREE PUBLISHERS
1700 Chattahoochee Avenue
Atlanta, Georgia 30318-2112

www.peachtree-online.com

Text and illustrations © 2002 Harry Horse

Illustrations created in pen and ink and watercolor
First published in Great Britain in 2002 by Penguin Books

Manufactured in China
10 9 8 7 6 5 4 3 2 1
First Edition

Library of Congress Cataloging-in-Publication Data
Horse, Harry.
   Little rabbit lost / written and illustrated by Harry Horse.
      p. cm.
Summary: On his birthday Little Rabbit thinks that he is now a big
rabbit, until he gets lost at the Rabbit World amusement park.
   ISBN 1-56145-273-4
   [1. Rabbits--Fiction. 2. Birthdays--Fiction. 3. Lost children--Fiction.
4. Amusement parks--Fiction.] I. Title.
PZ7.H7885 Li 2002
[E]--dc21
                                                      2002002697

Little Rabbit woke up and knew it was a special day. "It's my birthday," he said. "I'm not such a little rabbit any more!"

He hopped out of bed and found a wonderful pile of presents
and an enormous red balloon.

The whole family watched as he opened his presents.

"Happy birthday, Little Rabbit!" they cheered. "And one more surprise…"

"Tickets for Rabbit World. For all of us!" Little Rabbit had wanted to go to Rabbit World for as long as he could remember. He was *very* excited.

Mama packed a special birthday picnic,
and soon everyone was ready to go.

They set off for
Rabbit World with
Little Rabbit and his red
balloon leading the way.

Little Rabbit led them across the fields.
"Don't go too far!" called Papa.

"But it's my birthday and I'm a big rabbit now,"
shouted Little Rabbit. Then he ran ahead anyway.

Little Rabbit suddenly stopped at the top
of a hill and everyone caught up with him.
"Look!" said Little Rabbit. "It's Rabbit
World! It's huge!" And off he ran again.

On the signpost:
CARROT SPEEDBOATS
BOUNCY CASTLE
BIG HOPPER

When they were all inside Rabbit World,
Little Rabbit couldn't decide what to do first.
He wanted to go on everything at once.

"Don't go too far!" called Mama. "There are lots of rabbits here and you might get lost. Stay close."

"But it's my birthday and I'm a big rabbit now," said Little Rabbit. "I won't get lost."

Little Rabbit quickly ran off ahead, past the pirate ship and carrot speedboats. There was so much to see and do!

"Mama, can you push me on the big swings? Can I go on the jungle gym?"

"I'm sorry, Little Rabbit, but you're too small," said Mama. "You can go on the whirly slide though."

"That's for babies, Mama. It's my birthday and I'm a big rabbit now. I want to go on that!" said Little Rabbit, pointing…

...to the Big Hopper.

"I'm sorry, Little Rabbit, but you're much too small for that ride," said Mama. So Little Rabbit had to watch his brothers and sisters zoom past instead.

Little Rabbit soon got bored watching. "It's not fair," he said to himself. "It's my birthday and I *am* a big rabbit. Why can't I go on the really fun rides like everyone else?"

"Wow!" said Little Rabbit. "I wonder if my new rocket will fly that fast?"

"Hooray! A bouncy castle! Even *I'm* allowed to go on this." And so Little Rabbit clambered on and jumped and bounced and hopped until…

"Oh," said Little Rabbit.
"Where's Mama? And Papa?"
He suddenly felt as small
as he really was.

Little Rabbit asked some bigger rabbits, "Have you seen my mama?"

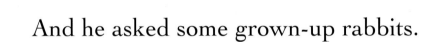
And he asked some grown-up rabbits.

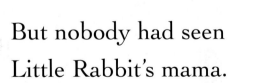

But nobody had seen Little Rabbit's mama.

"Has anyone seen my mama?" asked Little Rabbit.

Little Rabbit began to cry.
He was all alone and didn't
know what to do.

Other rabbits gathered
round, asking him lots
of questions. And then,
through all the voices
he heard…

"Little Rabbit! There you are! We've been so worried!"

It was Mama. "Thank goodness for your red balloon! I thought we'd never find you."

Little Rabbit was so happy he cried a bit more.

"I'm sorry, Mama. I *am* still your Little Rabbit. I'll stay close now," said Little Rabbit.

His mama gave him a great big hug. "Come on," she said. "I think we've all had enough of Rabbit World for one day."

The Rabbit family settled down to enjoy
Little Rabbit's birthday picnic. Little Rabbit
made sure he stayed very close to Mama.
"Just one last surprise…" said Mama.

"Happy birthday, Little Rabbit!"